For my courageous son, Will, for running in the right direction
Love always, Chris – CM

For Allie, Betty and Merle – ET

First published in Great Britain in 2001 by Bloomsbury Publishing Plc
38 Soho Square, London, W1V 5DF

A CIP catalogue record of this book is available from the British Library
ISBN 0 7475 5585 0

Designed by Sarah Hodder
Printed in Hong Kong by Wing King Tong

1 3 5 7 9 10 8 6 4 2

# RUN, RABBIT, RUN

## Christine Morton and Eleanor Taylor

BLOOMSBURY
CHILDREN'S
BOOKS

Rabbit hid inside his hole. His hidey-hole.
His tidy hole. His keep-your-nose-insidey hole.
'I'm hiding from something red,' said Rabbit.
'Is it the hen?' squeaked the mice.
'No, no, no,' said Rabbit. 'It's MUCH more dangerous than a *hen*!'

Rabbit hid inside a tree. A secret tree.
A green tree. A bet-I-can't-be-seen tree.
'I'm hiding from something hairy,' said Rabbit.
'Is it the horse?' said the birds.
'No, no, no,' said Rabbit. 'It's MUCH
more dangerous than a *horse*!'

Rabbit hid behind a sheep. A cuddly sheep. A snugly sheep.
A snug-as-a-bug-in-a-rugly sheep.
'I'm hiding from something with sharp teeth,' said Rabbit.
'Is it the farmer's new plough?' said the lambs.
'No, no, no – it's much more dangerous than a *plough*!'

Rabbit hid inside a tub. A wash tub.
A splosh tub. A get-inside-and-squash tub.
'I'm hiding from something with a tail,' said Rabbit.
'Is it the new black piglet?' said the geese.
'No, no, no – it's much more dangerous than a *piglet*!'

Rabbit hid in the barn. An old barn. A warm barn.
A shelter-from-a-storm barn.
'I'm hiding from something with a dirty white bib,' said Rabbit.
'Is it the farmers new billy goat?' said the cow.
'No, no, no – it's MUCH more dangerous than a *billy goat*!'

Inside the barn it was cool and dark. The door opened – cree-eak.
Something crept closer. Something red and hairy.
Something with teeth and a tail and a dirty white bib in front.
But it was too dark for Rabbit to see.

'Who is it?' said Rabbit. 'Is it the farmer, come to give me some carrots?'
'Oh no, no, no,' said a Very Sly Voice. 'I'm MUCH more dangerous
than the *farmer*.'

AND OUT JUMPED THE FOX

Run, Rabbit, Run! Run and jump and scrabble

Out of the barn

Past the billy goat

Through the cows

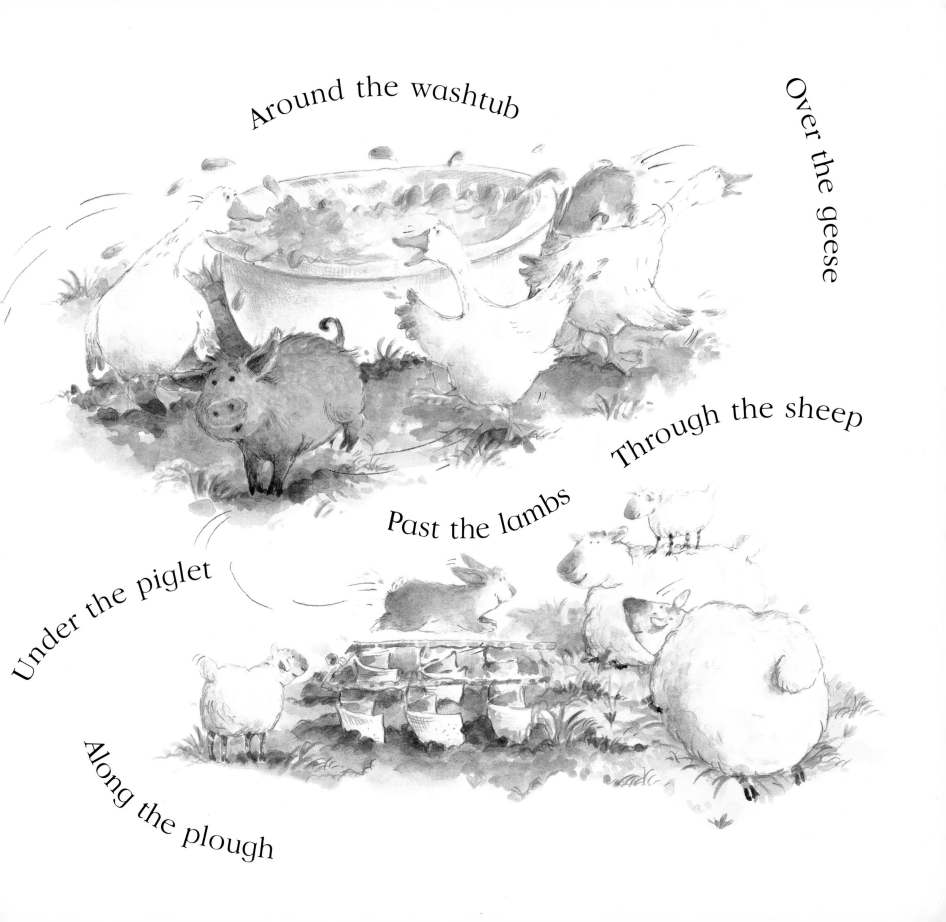

Around the washtub

Over the geese

Through the sheep

Past the lambs

Under the piglet

Along the plough

Under the horse

Over the birds

Past the tree

Over the hens

Around the mice

And-into-the-hole!

PHEW!

Then one cross whiskery eye peeped in.
And a nose went snuffle-snuffle-snuffle.
But Rabbit hid in his hole and smiled.
His hidey-hole. His tidy hole. His keep-your-nose-insidey hole.
Then Rabbit rolled over on to his back and had a good laugh
at the grumpy face.

'You may be red and hairy and have teeth and a tail
and a dirty white bib,' said Rabbit.
'But I can still run MUCH faster than you!'

Queen's Gate Junior School.

PB
MOR